Leave Taking

Lorraine Marwood

UQP

First published 2018 by University of Queensland Press
PO Box 6042, St Lucia, Queensland 4067 Australia
Reprinted 2019 (three times)

uqp.com.au
uqp@uqp.uq.edu.au

Cover design by Jo Hunt
Illustrations by Peter Carnavas
Author photograph by Kyle Marwood
Typeset in 13/22pt Adobe Garamond by Jo Hunt
Printed in Australia by McPherson's Printing Group

Australian Government | Australia Council for the Arts

The University of Queensland Press is assisted by the Australian Government through the Australia Council, its arts funding and advisory body.

MAY GIBBS Children's Literature Trust

Leave Taking was developed as part of a Creative Time Residential Fellowship provided by the May Gibbs Children's Literature Trust.

NATIONAL LIBRARY OF AUSTRALIA

A catalogue record for this book is available from the National Library of Australia

ISBN 978 0 7022 6011 7 (pbk)
ISBN 978 0 7022 6139 8 (epdf)
ISBN 978 0 7022 6140 4 (epub)
ISBN 978 0 7022 6141 1 (kindle)

University of Queensland Press uses papers that are natural, renewable and recyclable products made from wood grown in well-managed forests. The logging and manufacturing processes conform to the environmental regulations of the country of origin.

FSC www.fsc.org
MIX
Paper from responsible sources
FSC® C001695

To all those who have been touched
by cancer, take heart.

By the track

I shiver in my sleeping-bag.
There's dew on the grass,
and the faint silver of dawn,
but dark shadows hide the everyday
world outside my tent.

There's the first magpie call,
then
Dad slams the back door,
the motorbike revs.
It's cow-milking time,
and the sun is not even awake.

Dad yells, 'Morning Toby!' as he passes by,
and I smell exhaust fumes, sharp, strong.

It's every morning, every evening,
milking our herd,
150 cows trekking
from paddock to milking shed,
then back out to a new, fresh, juicy
paddock for the day.

I unzip the tent,
peer outside.
I am camping on the grass
near the farm track,
on our farm, once Pa's farm,
and his father's before that.

I look around as if
I've just landed
on this tiny piece of rural
planet Earth.
'Deep Well Farm' –
that's how it's always been known.

Once families came from all around
in horse-and-drays to bucket
clean water.
That's one of Pa's farm stories,
'How Our Farm was Named'.

'All covered up before my time,' said Pa.
'But the original well is somewhere
in that little orchard
behind the house.
My father showed me
how to divine for water.
Maybe I could show you and Leah,'
Pa had said.

'Yes, yes,' we'd shouted,
and even though Leah's
arms weren't strong,
we each had a forked twig
and held it just like Pa,

then walked up and down
the little row between the mulberry tree,
the peach tree, the apricot tree, the apple tree,
until Pa's twig moved and pointed down
like an arrow.
'Oh, that hurts my arm, all that water
energy. Perhaps, Toby, you should just have a go.
Not you Leah. Maybe when you're stronger …'
And Leah's face had gone stormy,
so Pa had held her twig too
and walked with her,
and the water energy had shaken
along her twig. 'You've inherited the skill, Leah.
You could be a water diviner,
but it's hard work. Although some people think
it's a joke.'

And we'd placed a big rock where the well
once was.

'It would take a lot of digging out.
Maybe if there's another
drought we could dig,' said Pa.
And we hadn't gone back to the old well
lately, not since Leah had to spend so much
time in hospital.
But Pa and I still talked
about our farm's namesake.
Maybe I will visit the site this morning,
have another go at water divining.
Maybe.

I hear the first cows
coming up the track.
Whoosh of urine –
walking always makes the cows' bladders active –
the stop and start
of the motorbike,
Dad chasing those straggler cows,

the tearaway cow,
bringing them down to the cowshed.
Morning milking time.

Trigger comes
to look in the tent,
to sniff for crickets
or chocolate crumbs left
over from my midnight feast.

'Help me cook breakfast,' I say.
I light a fire at the tent's front,
a little fire dug into the ground,
kept safe by a ring of rocks.
Twigs flare.
I find the frying pan.

'A sausage for you, two for me.
An egg as well, Trigger?'

Trigger licks his doggy lips.
'Alright, an egg it is.'
Sizzle noises,
eggshell cracking noises,
then I put bread on
a toasting fork.

But I remember not long ago,
it wasn't just Trigger and me,
but Leah too. Mum and Dad as well,
all of us together, cooking,
sitting, laughing,
throwing twigs on the fire.

We'd gone camping at One Tree Rock.
Just for one night; Pa milked the cows
the next morning so we could all go together.

'Family time for Leah,' Mum had said.

‘We’ll keep her warm, extra safe.’
And there was Leah toasting bread,
Leah melting marshmallows,
Leah making a song about
a campfire, about sparks and fairies
and eyes of coals and smoke
leaping into the morning light.
Mum and Dad laughed at her song,
telling her she was a born story maker …
That was maybe five months ago, not long before
Leah died and Mum had held her close
and whispered about the baby to come.

And I drop my bread,
my hand seems weak
remembering that camping time,
then I quickly pull the bread out of the ashes,
knock off tiny pieces of charcoal,
sticks and dust. I place it on the toasting
fork once more.

Machinery brrrs into life,
the rhythmical hiss and sigh
of milking machines.
The huge steel milk vat
purrs like a big-stomached cat
ready for endless thick milk.

The day has officially begun
with the first set of milking cups
on the first cow
who is always the leader
and is always first.
Cows are bossier and love routine
even more than my friend Emmy.
And the very last cow is always last too.

Now I explore this farm,
our family farm,

as if it's my first visit, like I'm a cousin
or a friend coming to our farm, learning,
seeing our family's treasures,
but I try to hide that it's really close
to the last time I will be able
to wander and remember how our farm
is right now.
Soon it will change
and another family will work things
out a different way, maybe pull down a building,
make a new laneway, build a new cowshed …
I don't know, but it won't be the same. It will
be their farm, no longer ours.

I walk to touch each hand-planted tree:
red gum, sugar gum, melaleuca,
bottlebrush, wattle. Mum grows all these trees
for farm shelter,
bird shelter,

ladder steps to the sky
for me.

Some trees hold my history:
my growing-up falls,
my tree house skills.
I touch the scars left by my building
and climb my favourite
tree just for fun.

Now up high I look across
the flat farmscape,
try not to see or remember the huge
'For Sale' sign hammered into the soil
near the fence of the paddock closest to the road,
and the bright red
'Sold' sign
plastered across it.

Mum and Dad had talked about selling,
about moving on, a fresh start, but I'd
said, 'No, no! What about Leah?'
And I'd shouted and shouted and run
to the haystack. Trigger had come too.
And he'd licked all my tears until I couldn't
cry anymore.
Then after a week or two had gone by,
somehow I'd grown used to the idea.
A little bit.

Then Dad had talked to me, shown me
the rolled-up map he'd drawn as a boy.
How he'd marked important spots around the farm
with little sketches and coloured them in
with pencils,
labelled them with names and hints of mysteries.

'Several generations of little stories,
yours now,' he'd said.

And I'd taken that map
and looked and looked, until I'd named it
'Leave Taking' and made my own version.

Leah would have liked that.
She liked all the places around the farm I liked.
I'd wanted Dad to tell her about the farm too
and Pa to tell her his stories. And they did,
often when she was in for a hospital stay;
the farm stories helped her to forget
about her pain,
about her tiredness.
Leah would have made a great farmer.
She was gentle. Dad said Leah was good
with calves,
with cows. Gentle is good for the milking shed.

I rub my eyes and look again
from up high
and see the silos

higher still than me.
The sheds are dotted
around: machinery,
calf sheds, storage sheds,
welding, mechanical repairs sheds
bursting with it-might-come-
in-handy odds and ends
accumulated over many years.

Yesterday, Dad began to sort
them into clearing sale lots.

Trigger is barking for me
to come down.
'Okay,' I say. 'We have to move camp
anyway.'

I have a plan to visit different
sites around the farm and camp
at each one before we shift.

It will be like a special goodbye tour,
my way, for Leah, for the farm
stories she didn't have time to hear.
I have my 'Leave Taking' map with me,
and I can add new labels for Leah's and my
farm history.

I've seen a spot from my treetop
lookout. A concreted corner
of the machinery shed.
I want to find my initials that I
wrote in the wet cement three
years ago.

But first I throw the breakfast scraps
to the magpies; I know them.
They don't swoop me, generations
have been born and lived here:
that big sugar gum over there
is their home nest.

'Just in case I don't get
another chance, goodbye,'
I say, then add,
'fly well and thanks.'
The words my grandma used to say,
every time she shook the tablecloth
out the back door
and the crumbs were scattered.

On the last word, I toss the scraps
and the magpies squawk and pounce.

I pull out the tent pegs
and start the packing up.
I move to
my new sleeping spot.

Trigger sniffs for mice.
'Chase them all out before
tonight,' I say.

Then I remember Dad and the cows,
look across to see the number
of cows left in the yard.
Last two line-ups of cows, the backing gate
moving down slowly.
It's my cue.
I change my sneakers for
gumboots, walk to the shed.

My job is hosing down
the manure,
all green and thick
from the yarded cows.
It covers every speckle of concrete.

There's a system, a rhythm,
and I power away the manure
in thick rivulets, directing
the flow towards the manure pit,
the manure pump on.

I had to show Leah how
to fire the hose so it sweeps
away the manure.
The hose was almost too thick
and heavy for Leah to hold. Even though
she was two years younger than me,
she wanted to share the jobs.
She was determined to do it.

Dad waves to me
from the pit of the milking shed.
It's too noisy to talk.
We wave and smile.
Co-cow workers.

Once the yard is clean
and the hose rolled up,
I head back to my new
camping spot.

I want to look for my initials
and see if Leah's are there too.
When the concrete was poured,
Leah had just begun to write letters.
She said, 'Wet cement and a stick
are like writing on the beach in the sand.'
Even though we'd only ever had one seaside
holiday, she remembered.
Leah made thick furry letters
and she had tried hard.

I search in the corner,
scratch at the dust with my boots.
Yes, like a little sandwich triangle
of concrete, crusty,
but there are my initials
and nearby Leah's initials
and a half-moon shape
as a smile.

I squat down and move my fingers
across Leah's initials, then jump up
quickly because Trigger is still sniffing,
whining at some
stacked hessian bags.

Snake, I think, snake
hunting for mice.

I run back to the cowshed.
Dad is just switching off
the machines, he's ready
to head back home for
breakfast.
'Snake,' I blubber out.
'Snake, in the machinery shed,
Trigger's there.'

'Get Trigger out,' orders Dad.

I remember one of our cats
getting a snake bite; I don't want
Trigger to die. I want to take
him to our new place, part of
my old life coming with me to the
new.

I call then, pull Trigger away,
my knees are shaky.
We run from the shed
just as Dad runs in.
Lucky the machinery shed is close
to the milking shed.
I hear Dad grunting,
pulling the bags back,
scraping, his boots scratching
and rasping on concrete.

Then silence.

'Dad, are you alright?
Dad?'

Dad reappears.

'Yes son, it was a brown snake,
fat from all the mice.
Those bags have got to go,
we'll put them on the bonfire
after breakfast.'

I remember Dad's dog White Tail.
He'd chase the cows home, follow Dad everywhere,
not let anyone else pat him. Just Dad,
and occasionally Mum.
Then one night when Dad was out
switching the irrigation channel to flow water
down another bay,
White Tail was bitten by a tiger snake.

And White Tail died, even though
we'd taken him to a vet an hour away.
And Dad cried.
First time we'd seen him cry, Leah and me.
But since then I've seen Dad cry a lot.
Even when he doesn't mean to cry,
he does.
So do I.

'Are you camping in here tonight?'
Dad is looking at my tent,
my sleeping-bag, my cooking gear,
and nodding.

'Yes.' I feel my eyes begin to prickle.
I don't want to tell him that I'm following his map,
have made a map of my own.
I'm not really sure why I'm doing it,
but it feels right,

and I have to do this before we leave for good
in less than a week. But Dad seems to know
what I'm thinking, why I'm doing it
even though I can't explain.

'Okay, that's fine son, just keep Trigger
with you. I'm sure we won't see
that brown snake again.'

Dad heads to the house
and I walk to the bonfire.
So many gardening scraps, bits of old
boxes, paper, anything that will burn,
to clean up the farm
ready for the new owners.

I helped Mum, a few days ago,
to sort through Leah's drawings;
she had so many.

‘We can’t keep everything,’ Mum explained,
and she’d smothered a sob.

So together we chose a little history of Leah’s life,
from her first preschool drawing
right through to the last,
when even her fingers
wouldn’t hold a pencil properly.
The rest we placed in a big cardboard box
and made sure it was in the heart of the bonfire.

The tractor is parked nearby
with the front-end loader attached.
Dad has pushed up the rubbish,
making the bonfire higher,
more compact.

I’ll help him later
with the hessian bags.

But now, I want to go
to the hayshed, remember
the times we made cubbies,
tunnels, our own private castles.

I wonder if the cubby Leah made
is still there or if the rain and winter
have knocked it away, or maybe Dad took
the bales to feed the cows. I don't know
but I'll check.

Trigger comes and nuzzles my hand.
Funny how my dog knows when I feel
sad.

Then I open the hayshed paddock gate.
Close it again. I remember once Leah
left the gate open and all the cows raced in
and ran round and round the hayshed
all night long.

Rubbing, knocking and nibbling,
snatching at hay in wild mouthfuls,
pooing everywhere and running in
an unstoppable flow of legs, swishing tails
and belching moos.

It was both funny and sad.
Dad was angry and Leah
was sorry.
My sister …
I brush the words away,
look at the old bales of hay
thrown on the ground,
too mouldy for the cows to eat.
Cows are fussy eaters,
or they might get sick.

This haystack area
is sometimes used to nurse a sick animal,
like a calf, or a cow, back to health.

Hard work.
I remember one time, one special calf.
I'd bring a bucket
of warm milk, a tube and rubber teat.
Try so hard to get it to drink,
rub its legs, make it stand,
but after a while it died.
I cried
so much.
'You tried hard son,'
Dad had said, 'but the calf needed to be
able to stand for longer, to drink more milk.
A sick calf takes a lot of attention and care.'
And Dad had ruffled my hair.

Farms are for new life
and new death.
We know.

Trigger is bounding up the bales,
they are wide, thick steps
but tricky steps.
A bale could be soft, broken,
and Trigger could fall down to the next layer.

Trigger is always full of energy;
brown kelpies are like that. He loves
chasing, running, exploring.
All these things he can do all day
if he wants to,
on a farm.

He's sniffing again.
How many mice live
in this hayshed, I wonder?

I follow, I want to see over
the farm, the land is flat.

Trigger sits with me,
wanting me to scratch his ears.

I remember Leah climbing
these hay bales, looking for the right layer
to change and switch the small bales
until they made a house shape.
'Don't move too many bales,'
Dad had warned,
'they could cave in,
smother you.'
So Leah had climbed back down
to the bottom two layers,
and I'd helped push, shove,
pull those bales to where Leah directed.

Jaxon had been over that day,
and we'd each made a little room
and played pirates racing from
top to bottom of the hay bales.

Our arms and legs were scratchy afterwards
and Leah's little arms had been bleeding,
so Mum had quietly said, 'No more moving
the bales, Leah. Take a rug for your house
next time.' But there had been no next
time for Leah and our cubby
had been knocked down
by the front-end loader, by the weather.
Luckily Leah had taken a photo that day
of our cubby, and each time I see the photo
it makes me smile.

Trigger nudges me.
I see a wedge-tailed eagle
soaring up above;
maybe it sees mice too,
or a hare.

I hear Dad's motorbike rev again;
he's out to check on the cows,

see if they got to the day paddock
alright.
Then I see a small spiral cloud
coming down
the dirt road beside our farm.
A ute passing,
dust tracking its
progress like a light flashing.

The blue wrens dart for insects
several bales away.
I am quiet,
steady, watching.

The wind makes little scurries
in the loose straw
right down below
at the base of the haystack,
and I sigh.

I don't understand how we can leave
this farm. I don't.
But I'm trying.
Funny, suddenly there are lots
of things I don't understand.
At least here, leaning on the highest hay bales
with Trigger, looking, feeling
the softness of summers past,
imagining Leah with me,
I can try.

The blue wrens dart
away.
Trigger looks at me with mournful eyes.
Does Trigger know we are leaving too?

'Come on back to the machinery shed,
we've got some sorting to do,'
I tell him.

In the machinery shed

I like this sorting,
well, that's one
good thing that comes from selling,
getting ready for the clearing sale.

Dad has boxes of useful nails, bolts,
screws, all jumbled together,
and I love to sort them
into the same sizes, new or old.
I find other trays,
heavy cardboard boxes,
keep sorting, try not to think
too much.

Mum comes and peers in;
she's looking for Dad

and says, 'Wish you were able to sort
them out years ago …
but you would have been too young.'

She looks at me, then smiles.
'You probably would have done
a good job then as well.
Lucky it's school holidays, Toby.
You've missed so much school this year …'
And there is a catch in Mum's voice.
She stops, wipes her eyes
and says,
'Tell Dad I'm looking
for him, if you see him before I do.'

Mum gives me a small hug.
Lately she wants to hug me every time
she sees me.
A hug good morning
and a hug goodnight are enough really.

But then I look at Trigger
and I know I hug him a lot more lately.
And he doesn't mind at all.
So perhaps I'd better like hugs more.
For Mum.

My fingers are getting greasy
and my tummy is rumbling.
'Morning tea surely,' I say to Trigger.
He wags his tail.
Anything I say
is good tail-wagging material,
except if I growl and that's not often,
well, not much anymore now
he's no longer a puppy.
I remember a time when he chewed
everybody's boots at the back door,
and he chased the chooks
when they were let out of a morning.

Chooks are not hunted on our farm,
except by foxes and if a fox comes
close to the house at night-time,
Trigger howls.

I run back to the house.
Rush inside, grab an apple,
some biscuits, water and maybe
some grapes if there are any left.

I think of how much Leah liked grapes
and stop right on the spot.
It hurts to remember special things
about Leah.
Now I have a tummy ache.
How can I stop these thoughts?
Is that wrong?
I don't know.
Wish my pa still lived here,
I could ask him.

Dad is inside again and making coffee.
Mum and Dad are talking,
I hear snatches:
'They will come for a look tomorrow.
See if more fencing needs to be done
in the bull paddock. They have prize bulls now.
Look at the pumps, look at some of the machinery
we are selling. They might make an offer before
the clearing sale.'

I don't want to hear any more.
I find a bag to put my food in
and jog outside again.
'They are coming,' I chant,
'I don't have much time left,' I chant.
I run back to the machinery shed,
my morning tea bumping along.

Trigger is jogging also. He waits while
I find the biscuits. Sits when I show him one,

then wolfs it down before I've even
found one for myself.
I sit on an upturned crate
and drink water, munch an apple,
look at the sorting I've already done
and the pile of broken bits and pieces
that probably need to be thrown out,
but I'll have to ask Dad first.

I tidy away my morning tea and slowly begin
to sort again, and that's when I find the project
Leah and I did last year. Hammering nails
into wood and then looping thread around
the nails to make a picture.
Leah was clever at this. Her picture is a heart
and I can't help it, tears just come.

I put Leah's picture up on Dad's wide bench.
'We'll take this with us,' I tell Trigger.

He wags his tail. It's good having a friend
who approves of everything you say.

I want to go outside,
I've had enough of sorting.
I have the chooks to feed.
And the silky bantam
to watch;
she might have hatched more chickens.

I take the apple core;
chooks are always hungry.
I have to check their water
and their pellets.
Later, I'll go back and collect the eggs.
We don't need so many eggs now.

I think we can take the bantams to our new place.
Leah would have liked that.

Trigger knows where we're heading.
It's like he smells feathers and dust
and the scrap bucket as soon as we
take the short cut past the bonfire
and the sugar gums to the chook house.
Or maybe he can hear them scratching
and the contented way they sing and mutter
when they're hunting in the grass.

I say, 'Steady now,
don't frighten the chooks.'
Trigger pants and slobbers.
I know that I can't completely trust him;
he wants to chase them.

The hens are chortling, the dust flying
as they enjoy their day.
They always race out when I prop open the door
first thing in the morning.
I remember making this chook house from

old fencing wire, mesh, an old door, tin.
Dad helped.
It was fun.
We haven't done anything like that for …
I shut my eyes, will my mind
not to think.
Then I remember how we scratched
our initials in the concrete
of the machinery shed.

And now I want to paint my initials on the beam
of the chook house door.
To make some history of my own.
There are some half-empty tins
of paint I found when I was sorting.
'Come on Trigger,' I call. Can't leave him
here alone.
We run back to the machinery shed.
I grab the red paint, a small tin
of yellow paint, a tiny brush.

'Come on Trigger,' I yell again
as I head back to the chook house.
He thinks it's a game; his pink tongue
hanging out, ears back, he runs, runs
and tries to chase the big black rooster.
'No,' I shout.
'Stop,' I shout.
And Trigger pulls up, sits down
panting, looking back at me. Waiting.

'Ah Trigger, don't chase the chooks,' I growl.
I pull over a stump of wood,
open the red can, stir the paint with a stick,
dip in the brush, stand on the log
and reach to write my initials.

Then I wipe the brush on the grass
and dip it in the yellow paint.
I write Leah's initials and a curve for a smile.
There, it's done.

Time to check on the silky bantam.
I've made a little nesting room
for her (with Dad's help)
by putting up mesh and a frame
on the back of the old outside toilet.
There's plenty of straw to make
a warm nest.
Two days ago, I counted six eggs.
I remember Mum answering Leah's questions.
'Clucky bantams,' Mum had called them,
'always wanting to go broody.'
'What's broody?' Leah had asked.
'When a hen wants to sit and hatch eggs,
not lay them each day.
Count how many days that bantam sits
on the nest, then watch for a surprise,'
Mum had said.

I look at a spot lower than me
on the door post and I can just faintly see

the marks Leah wrote as she
counted twenty-one days.
Leah had squealed with joy
at the chicks.

Will I see chicks today?

Yes, I hear the peep, peep of chickens
and there I see a tiny puffball of gold,
then another and another peering from under
the thick feathers of the mother bantam.

'Yay!' I shout. 'Six chicks!'
Leah would love to hold one chick, in her tiny
thin hand, like she did the last time
a bantam went broody.

I check on the water, the feed for the bantam
in her nesting pen,
then go back to the main pen.

I know we will take some chooks with us
and leave others.

'Goodbye chook house,' I whisper.

I have time to visit the deep well site.
See if our big rock is still there,
the one we helped Pa put in place
to mark the site of the long-ago
freshwater well.

I take the two paint cans with me
and a broken piece of wood from
a crate as a marker, of sorts.

I sit on the big rock, stir the red paint
and write 'Deep Well' on the wood,
and alongside it draw
a yellow smile.
Then I push it into the moist soil.

There! Another piece of my and Leah's
farm history.

'Goodbye hidden deep well,' I say.

I'm not really brave alone in the machinery shed for the night. Mum comes to check on me just as the sky turns into darkest blue with its own thousands of pinpricks of starlight.

'Dad told me about the snake,' she said.
'I know you'll be fine with Trigger.
But the back door will be left unlocked
if you change your mind.'
Mum hugs me and somehow
I know she also knows about
my goodbyes.

Trigger wags his tail.
He wants a hug too.
'The two cats are coming to share the shed with you. Good to keep mice away, good to keep snakes away as well,' says Mum.
I nod and yawn.
Saying goodbye is tiring work.

Next to Pa's old truck

It's so early, but I feel as if I've had a good sleep,
even though concrete
is harder on my back than the earth.
The two cats are
rolled up next to me, warm, soft.
One purrs as if she knows I am now awake.
'Shelley,' I whisper.
That's the name Leah gave to her cat.

Tilly stretches and her claws
graze Trigger
who is rolled next to me too.

'Woof!' he gives a throaty startled bark,
and then I hear the motorbike.

Another day starts,
another day closer to leaving.
Today I'm too lazy to cook my own breakfast,
not eggs and sausages, just toast
cooked in the toaster in the kitchen.
After breakfast
I want to set my tent up
near the old truck.
Pa's old truck,
across from the hayshed.
Left there the last time its engine roared
to life. Not sure when that was,
but I can ask Pa;
he knows all about the farm
history stretching
way back.

'Good job,' Dad says
as he looks in the machinery shed
at my sorting.
'Reckon those boxes will sell well at the clearing
sale.'
I smile. I can still smile.

'Is Pa coming soon?' I ask.
Dad looks at my tent already packed up
and asks instead,
'Where to next?'
'Down by the old truck,' I say.
Dad nods and adds, 'It is a good time for Pa
to come then. He can tell you all about that truck.
He will be here soon.'

Suddenly it seems too quiet now.
Just me in the family,
no one to play with. I even miss Leah's jokes,
her little tricks … especially her April Fools' jokes.

She loved teasing me at breakfast.
Once she tricked me by saying, 'We have new
breakfast cereal that is
both crunchy and soft.'
'Rubbish, how can that be?' I'd asked,
not knowing she'd carefully cut up marshmallows
and mixed them with cornflakes.
'Ha! Big April fool!' she'd squealed when I'd helped
myself to a big bowl of her special joke mixture.

I don't want my friends around yet.
They ask silly questions,
think I might get sick like Leah,
or they might catch the sickness.
I know they don't know what to say
or their words come out all wrong
and sharp.

I don't know what to say either,
so no one says anything

and they keep away from me.
Only Emmy and Jaxon try,
as if they have rehearsed a speech
for a school play.
'Are you sad?' they ask.
'What do you do by yourself now?' they ask.
Silly questions.
Of course I'm sad.
Of course I'm lonely.
Then Emmy brought me grapes
in her lunch box
and made an 'I'm sorry' card.

That helped a lot.
But there is so much
inside me that hurts,
so doing this map of goodbye
makes me feel
a bit more like the Toby
I was when I was a big brother.

I put all my gear into a trolley I've made.
Pull it along the dirt track
into the hayshed paddock,
over to the old rusted truck.
The truck was red once.
Still has Pa's farm name on the side
and a cool lever you can lift as an indicator
like a rod with a hand on the end.

I climb into the driver's seat, even though
the leather is ripped and there are probably
mice or spiders.
Trigger jumps up wanting to see in,
wanting to be a cattle dog
on a ute tray.

The truck door groans and squeaks
as I push it open again.
I think about the big step out the door

onto the ground,
then look in the door pocket,
find pieces of paper
Leah wrote on for our last game here.

'To' and 'From' pieces of paper
to make bus tickets:
'From our farm to market'
'From our farm to town'
'From our farm to the moon'.
Silly Leah,
as if our truck could fly!
It wouldn't even go on a road now.
The tyres are worn out, ripped,
the tray is rusted and wild oats are growing
up through the wooden slats.

I push myself from the driver's seat,
back down to the long grass,

close the truck door.
I squirt water from my water bottle
on the windscreen, write my name
on the muddy dust,
then crookedly write
'To the moon'.

I find a clear, grassy area to pitch my tent.
I hammer in the pegs. Tie the ropes.
Set up my sleeping-bag,
make a little fire pit.

Now for exploring and saying goodbye.
Ha! Tilly and Shelley are here too,
wanting me to poke and prod around;
maybe I might disturb more mice, so the
cats get ready to hunt.

Trigger ignores them and goes sniffing,
digging, chasing.

There goes a hare!
There goes Trigger!
Will there be places for Trigger
to run on our next farm?

I look in my tent for my camera,
well, it's Leah's.
She loved taking photos.
I snap the truck from all angles.
It's a mystery
and I make my own history for it.

But it feels too sad using Leah's camera.
I'll only use it for the truck.
I can draw the rest on the map.

Maybe the truck took Pa's prize Jersey cows
to the Royal Show; I know he had prize cows.
Maybe it carted square bales
to another farm for hungry cattle,

maybe it took Grandma and my dad
along with Pa on market days
and Grandma went shopping, bought
a new dressing table, or a new bed for Dad.

Ha! Pa had better hurry and tell me the real history.

I'm hungry again.
I call, 'Trigger!'
He's a long way off.
'TTTriGGGer,' I yell.

Then I see someone walking down
the dirt track
and Trigger is jumping up,
wagging his tail furiously.
'Pa!' I shout.
'Pa! Over here!'
And I can't help it,
tears trickle down again.

I don't wait but charge off
to meet him.
The cats aren't interested;
they lie in the sun.

'How's my boy?' yells Pa as we get closer.
And the tears become
a tiny waterfall.
I'm crying and running
and hiccuping
all mixed into one.
Trigger stops jumping and stands still.
It's like he doesn't know me;
how could he? All my sadness
for Leah is turning me into a stranger.

'That's it Toby, let it go,' and Pa is hugging me tight.
And I'm sure Pa is crying too.
I know that crying gives me a headache
and the reddest eyes ever.

But it's like a big lump in my chest
is free.
'Why did Leah have to die, Pa?' I ask.
Silly, stupid question.
'Why Leah? Will I get cancer too?'

'Ah! Come on over to the truck,
we're nearly there,
we'll have a seat on this old log.
Come on, here's a handkerchief,
let's mop up and then we can talk.'

Trigger recognises me again
and comes, tail wagging,
putting his head in my lap.

Pa doesn't say anything for a while, not until
I've stopped hiccuping.

'It's good to let all that grief out,' he says.
'It's going to take a long time to build a family
again.'
I don't really know what Pa means, but I nod.

'And one way your mum and dad
have worked out their sadness
is to shift to a new farm.
Smaller, a new district,
but it will help.
A new baby coming will help too.

'None of us want to forget Leah,
and wish she was here
every single moment
of every day.
We can't bring her back,
but we can live for her.'

I'm warm with Pa's arms still around me
and his words are like
a bedtime story:
they sound right, feel right,
but I still don't understand them
and I'm still angry.
Angry that Leah died.
'Why couldn't they give her more chemo?' I ask.

'Because her little body had had enough.
Oh Toby, she is at peace now. Truly.'

We sit for a while longer
then the cats come close,
chasing each other,
too close to Trigger.
He likes his personal space,
as Mum calls it. So he snaps at Shelley
and Shelley spits back.

Then there are growls, wailings,
and Pa and I jump up.
'Enough!' shouts Pa, and the animals stop
immediately.

'Just a bit of fun,' I say.
'The cats do like Trigger,
not sure Trigger likes them though.'

Pa is looking inside my tent.

'Looks snug.
I like your cooking pit too.
Will I fill the billy for a cup of tea?
I have our lunch here.'
And Pa pulls a big brown bag
out of his coat pocket.
'Chops, some bananas to fry, tomatoes
and a potato to cut up for chips.'

'Yum,' I say.
'I'll just get some more sticks and leaves.'
And together Pa and I find offcuts
and branches
of old wood to build our fire.
There are always handy things lying around
on a farm.

The smoke smells like eucalyptus
and the fire begins to bank into some coals.
'Where's that hotplate?' asks Pa.
We rub it down with a little container of oil
that Pa has in his parcel.

Then we begin peeling the potato,
slicing it into small flat chips and setting
them cooking,
next frying the chops,
and while all that is sizzling away,
putting tea and gumleaves
into the billy of water.

Trigger is watching us, sniffing the air,
making little growls of joy. The cats have
gone back to exploring the hay bales.
They are poking in the small gaps between the
ends of bales, using their paws to prod.
'Like dry fishing for mice,' laughs Pa
as he watches them.

'Help me pull that log closer to the fire.
I know you want to find out some more
about the old red truck, and we have time
before lunch.'

Pa stirs the fire a bit, moves the hotplate a bit
and he starts talking.
'That truck was second-hand
when I bought it.
We needed a truck to cart bales
from the paddock to the hayshed.
The bales were small in those days.
It also had a crate we could put on
the back of the tray
to take pigs and calves to market.'

'Pigs!' I say.
'Yes, all the milk was separated into cream
for the factory and the leftover milk fed the pigs.
Look behind us,
there are some of the old pig sties
I built with my father, your great-grandfather.
No need for pigs now. The milk tanker takes
whole milk, all the day's milk.'

I'm thinking. 'Will you miss this farm then,
when the O'Briens take it on?'

'Yes and no. I have memories,
good memories that no farm sale
can take away.
It's time to let someone else have a go.
And that's tricky Toby,
knowing when to leave.
It's very hard. But afterwards you know it's right.
I'm sure the sale of the farm and the shift will feel
right sooner than you think.
But back to my story …

'You know once upon a time this truck,
before I bought it,
carted fish from the city market
to our town,
so it's had lots of adventures.

But eventually
it needed too much repair work
and I needed a bigger truck.
That was just before your dad
came back to work the farm with your mum.
Before you and Leah were born.
We left it here near the hayshed,
thinking we'd get it fixed up,
use it again,
but we never did.

'Oh! I think our lunch is cooked. Plates?' asks Pa.
And I look in my backpack.
I find plates, mugs, knives, forks.

'And I have salt, a little bit of homemade sauce,
a towel and some milk,' says Pa.

Pa lifts the hotplate and settles it on some grass.
He dishes out the meal.

Sets aside a small chop for Trigger.
'It has to cool first.
Patience Trigger,' he says.

Then the blue wrens flitter nearby.
Pa throws a tiny scrap.
A magpie comes, then its mate.

'If we're not careful
we'll have all sorts of wildlife around us,
and we don't want the unwelcome visitor
you had yesterday.'
Pa gives me a wink.

'Ah! Trigger, your lunch is cool enough to eat now
and the cats can have my scraps. Do you want
to take these pieces to Shelley and Tilly?' asks Pa.

I like how my pa knows the cats' names.
Leah would have liked it too.

'Time for a mug of tea.' Pa stirs
the gumleaves with a twig,
puts the lid back on and swings the whole
billy around and around.

'Takes practice, that does,' he laughs.

'Let me show you some of the features
of the truck,'
suggests Pa,
as we wipe the plates on the grass
and pour the rest of the billy tea over them.

'You know about the signals?'
I nod and work them.
Then Pa explains all the different knobs.
'No computer programming in this.
Made it easier for us to do repairs
so far out from town.

Guess this will go in the clearing
sale too?'

I nod.
'Good. Someone might love doing up
this old truck.'

'I'm going back to the house now Toby.
Leave you to your goodbyes.'

Funny, even Pa knows about my secret plan.

'What about you?' I blurt out,
suddenly sad again.

'Oh, I said my goodbyes
to this place years ago
when your grandma and I left for retirement.
It's your turn now.'

I wave as Pa turns back once more
before the track curves
and the shelter trees we planted
hide him from sight.

I climb into the truck cabin again and try
to remember the purpose of the knobs
and the meaning
of the dials on the dashboard.

Then I climb back out and say,
'Goodbye red truck.'

Tonight it will be special to sleep nearby
and think about pigs grunting
and fish, silver as ice,
packed on the back of the old red truck.

On Memorial Hill

The days are running out before the clearing sale,
before the bonfire
and before all our family and friends
come to say goodbye.

I have one last place I want to pitch my tent.

Leah and I made up a name for it:
Memorial Hill.
On a flatland farm, a little hill is exciting,
means we can run up, slide down
on old, squashed cardboard boxes.

Memorial Hill is right at the back of our house,
near the old outside toilet,

where the bantams are now.
And over the fence is the dam
that used to provide water for the garden.
So Dad reckons that the dirt
was dumped there to make a hill
when the earth was scooped out
for the dam.

The hill is where Leah and I made little graves
for our pets or for a small parrot or kingfisher
we found dead on the farm.
We made little circles of stones and put up crosses.
Here is where Dad's old dog Streak is buried
and his last dog White Tail
and the mother cat
of our kittens.

Here are the sugar gums
planted by Pa's grandmother.

So they are very old.
Galahs nest here
around Christmas time
and the ground is covered
in old gumnuts and leaves.

This place is quiet, special.

Maybe Leah would have liked
to have been buried here.
But she has her own place near our grandma.
The hill is where I feel close to Leah.
How can I say goodbye to this place?
How?
Leah was just a toddler when Grandma died
and Pa came to live with us for a while.
But I remember Grandma well.
She was always drawing and singing;
maybe that's where Leah got her talents.

Trigger is already snuffling in the leaves.
He ignores, for once, the chooks
scratching nearby.
They love this place too.
Lots of beetles
and grubs and worms to eat.

I walk around the little pet graves,
work out where I can pitch my tent.
Wonder where Pa buried
his pets,
when he was a boy.

I can hardly remember the mother cat
and suddenly
I have a terrible thought:
Will I remember Leah?
I have photographs,
I have her handmade birthday cards,
our games together.

I will remember.

I find a spot right at the highest point
of the little hill
and begin hammering in the pegs.
It's hard work.
The hill is dry; all the tree roots underneath
have taken all the moisture and spread thickly
like an underground web,
searching for even more moisture.
But I get there.
I'm sweaty.
I finish putting up the tent.

Straight away, a gumnut lands plonk
on the plastic roof.
Oh well, it might be a noisy night.
I look out as far as I can see,
say goodbye to the paddocks,
the dam, Memorial Hill itself.

But never goodbye to Leah;
what we remember and know will
come with us.

I decide to collect some of the gumnuts.
I know if I put them in a paper bag
like Mum does, then tiny pepper-like seeds
will fall out and maybe Mum will show me
how to grow sugar gums on our new farm.

I'm hungry again,
and I'm certain Mum will be baking,
getting ready for the big bonfire night,
ready for the clearing sale.
I love smelling biscuits
or muffins cooking, and Mum
cooks a lot.
Not Leah's favourite of lemon
meringue pie anymore,
but Dad's favourites and mine.

'Need help?' I ask. What I really mean is:
Are there any spare crumbs or bowls to lick?
Mum nods, hands me
an Anzac biscuit and a jam drop biscuit.
Feast!

'How are the goodbyes going?' she asks
as she spoons mixture into muffin pans.
I haven't told anyone
but they all seem to know.
'And the camping? Where are you tonight?'

'Good,' I mumble. 'Nearly done.'
'Memorial Hill,' is all I say in answer
to her last question.

'Good,' Mum echoes, 'then you can start packing
again.'

Packing! I nearly choke.
'I know it's hard Toby, but it has to be done.
I have put some cardboard boxes in your bedroom.
You only packed your old toys before.
Just about everything has to be packed now.
You might find something to put
in the clearing sale in two days' time.
When you sort your things out.'

Mum smiles and hugs me.
'And Toby, will you help me with Leah's things?
I want to take her pencils, her little diaries,
some of her toys. You will know what to keep
better than me. Dad will help too. All together.'

Mum stops and tries to wipe her eyes
with floury fingers.
'Sorry Toby,' and Mum runs for the bathroom.
I can hear her crying and the water running
as she washes her hands.

'Okay Mum,' I call to her.
'I have to feed the chooks,
see the new chicks.
Be back later.'

Too much happening.

Too much.

But I go out again,
talk to Trigger,
think about Leah,
maybe sort some more bits and pieces for Dad
after I've done the chooks.

Pa waves from the machinery shed
when he sees me.
He's helping Dad sort out machinery.
After all,
some of it is Pa's very old stuff.

Already Pa and Dad have begun
to set up auction lots around
the back of the machinery shed.

And this afternoon they are using the tractor
to pull the red
truck closer too.

The bonfire has grown.
It's tall and wide.
Dad is putting thick logs
a bit of a way off, but still near the bonfire,
for seats.
He is finding more rubbish
as he and Pa work in the machinery shed.

A big BBQ is set up, ready for when
we have dinner on our last night on the farm.

There will be family and friends
from all around.
Coming to say goodbye,
wish us well,
remember Leah too,
chat about the times we've had here.
Last time we had a crowd it was after the funeral.
Well, there will be lots of people here
for the clearing sale,
but they might be mainly strangers, buyers
and perhaps stickybeaks too.
Too hard to talk then,
but later,
when it's time for the last goodbye,
Jaxon might like to jump on the trampoline
with me, or look at the bantam chicks …

I have to go and sit in my tent.
Everything is moving too fast now,

goodbyes will be shortened. Our time here
is quickly ending. A new farm, a new home;
smaller without Leah.
Different.
Sad, but I remember
what Pa said: To live is to remember Leah.

And I wipe my tears;
they just keep coming
without me even noticing sometimes.
Trigger licks my face, brings his favourite stick
for me to throw, nudges and nudges until I say:
'Alright Trigger, here, fetch.'
And he fetches and begs for me to throw
it again and again, until I'm smiling
at the way he scoops up the stick and charges back.
Then, just like that, Trigger has had enough
and lies down.
I think I'll lie down too
for a bit.

There's a shower of gumnuts
on the roof of my tent.
I wake up and it's late afternoon.
I can't work out where
I am, but remember it will be time to hose
down the cow yard soon.

I race over to the back door,
pull on my boots.
Both the cats and Trigger follow me
to the cowshed.
Pa's ute is gone.
There are only a few rows of cows
left to be milked.
Dad waves as he fetches another lot of cows
to line up.

I wait until the yard is empty,
pull up the backing gate.
Drag the thick hose right up to the end
of the concrete
and begin.
I remember again Leah taking turns with this job;
she always helped, especially with the calves.
I know on the next farm
we will only have cattle and sheep,
no dairy cows.
Different again.
Things change.
So much.
I know this now.

Mum, Dad and Pa are going through
the clearing sale lists
printed out from the computer.

We've had our dinner
and I'm helping to dry the dishes.
'Toby, are you still sleeping in your tent tonight?'
asks Mum.
I nod.
'Could be noisy under those sugar gums,' she adds.
'That's fine.' I smother a yawn. I'm so tired,
so tired.

Mum hugs me, wet tea towel and all. Kisses me.
Dad and Pa say goodnight as I take my torch,
push open the back door
and see Trigger waiting.

Outside the sky is like a Christmas pageant,
all that silver starlight.
I point the torch ahead
and catch the sudden thick flight
of an owl.

I hear the echo of a car on the road,
paddocks away. The wind stirs
the sugar gum leaves and the gumnuts plink
in a sudden, drumming flurry.

I put my torch down, fling my arms out wide,
look up to the sky and try to give this moment
one huge final hug.
'Goodbye farm night.' Then I pick up
my torch again, crawl into my tent,
my sleeping-bag.
Trigger crawls in too.

I listen to the night sounds
as if it's my own private concert,
until my tiredness
blots everything out.

It's clearing sale day.

Dad gets the cows in earlier than usual.
They grumble. Really.
Flick tails, butt one another,
charge in a different direction
to the motorbike.
Trigger knows everything is out of order
and barks. He's not a working dog; even though
he's a kelpie,
he failed his working-dog trial.
Some dogs don't make the grade,
Dad had said, and I begged him to keep Trigger,
my dog, my farm dog.
I'd pleaded and Dad had given in.
Of course, even the cows know
he's not a working dog and take no notice,
moo louder.

Last night Dad said, 'The auctioneers will be here
early.
I'll need your help Toby.
Pa will come too.'

Even before I roll the hose back up
from washing the yard, the first ute
arrives, then another.
The local CWA ladies
are catering and will use
the kitchen to prepare sandwiches.
All the power points in the machinery shed
are in use with the auctioneer's computers
and electronic equipment.
Little trestle tables spring up with labels
like registration, payment, enquiries.
There are clipboards, pens and brochures
typed up by the auctioneering company.
I sigh as I read the list of

all our goods, then watch as a man
puts lot numbers in front
of each pile of equipment or box.
'Tom Elliot's my name,' he says and shakes
my hand.

Pa is directing utes and cars
to the house paddock to park.
I see people I know. I half-wave,
half-hide.

'Here Toby,' Dad calls.
And I help place more boxes
from the machinery shed
in rows wide enough for people
to walk between.
Smaller items are in the machinery shed,
bigger items are outside.
There are so many boxes.

Soon there are more people
than dairy cows.

'There's the O'Brien family,' says Dad
and waves.

The auctioneer gets up on
the back of the old red truck.
'Hope he doesn't fall through,'
I mutter.

'Ladies and gentlemen, it's
time to begin the sale of a lifetime,
of a generation …'
I block my ears, go to my tree house,
climb till I am invisible behind
gumleaves.
I have my own secret place
to watch as the auctioneer
raises his voice and that man,

Tom Elliot, stands beside him
and scans the crowd for bids.
'Sold! Going, going! Sold!'
The words are repeated, the crowd moves
along the rows. Then slowly
utes back up, load their goods
and empty spaces appear.

People sit on hay bales
with mugs of tea, plates of sandwiches
and cakes.
Trigger whines for me to come down,
but I can't, not yet.
Pa waves once, Mum looks for me,
waves too, then the auctioneer
points to the old red truck he is standing on.
Bidding starts. 'Sold!' he shouts,
and someone brings in a bigger truck
with its own mini-crane and the old red truck
is winched onto the buyer's vehicle.

‘Goodbye, goodbye,’ I whisper,
and I let my head rest
on my folded arms.

Strangers and friends mill around
Dad, Pa and Mum, then the dust drifts
again as cars, utes, trucks leave,
piggybacking parts of our life.

‘Oh Leah,’ I whisper, ‘it’s sad
but you would have liked spying
on it all from up here.’

Goodbye Deep Well Farm

Pa is here early the next morning.
He's brought more chairs, and a table.
Then he keeps working in the machinery shed.
I go and help.
'Lots of bits and pieces that people didn't want
have been left behind,' he laughs.

'Pa,' I ask, 'how did you get used to leaving?'

'Hmm, I suppose your grandma and I
knew it was coming.
It gave us more time to do some travelling,
some hobbies.

We were happy here and happy
when your dad and mum
took over the work.
Perhaps I would have liked you or Leah
to take over too. But things change.
The O'Briens and their extended family will look
after the farm.'

'Will you come to our new farm?' I ask.
'It won't have milking cows.'

'Yes, I'll have to stay a few nights then,
it's a long way away.
Closer to your mum's family.
That will be good.
The cats, chooks and of course Trigger
will go with you,
and some of your dad's beef cattle,
so not everything has been sold.

And the tractors will go too.'

I nod. It's beginning to sound a little bit exciting.
Cousins I hardly know to meet,
a new school, new farm.

'But will we forget Leah?' I blurt out.
And the tears spring again.
'Of course not, Toby.
Listen, Leah is here in our hearts
and up here in our memories.
And on every special occasion
we'll remember her.' And Pa holds me tight.

'Come on, we've earned some morning tea
and I hear that your mum has had a big baking day.'
We put our boots at the back door,
wash our hands,
and Pa always combs his hair as well.

We help Mum with the coffee,
pile biscuits on plates.
'Not too many,' says Mum. 'We'll need some for tonight.'
'Lots coming?' asks Pa.
'Not sure, but expect a few. It's the final goodbye really.'
"That will be hard,' says Pa.
Mum nods.

We eat in silence, then Pa goes back to the shed
and I help Mum cut up carrots,
cabbage, celery, tomatoes, radishes.
'Salads for our BBQ tonight,' explains Mum.
'Are you happy to see some of your friends Toby?'
Mum looks at me closely.
I nod. I know it will be part of my goodbyes.
'At least there will be a huge bonfire
and Uncle Samuel will bring his guitar,' I say.
Then Mum gives me a hug.

I remember the last time Uncle Samuel came to
our farm. Leah was in bed recovering
from her latest round of chemo
and Uncle Samuel sang to her, even made up
little jingles about Shelley and Tilly.
That made Leah laugh. We all heard that
laughter and I try to recall it now, but all
I hear are the funny songs Uncle Samuel loves
making up.

'We'll never forget Leah.
Never,' says Mum as if she is also remembering
Leah's laugh.
'I think Dad will be glad to have his brother here
too,' adds Mum.
'Uncle Samuel always gets a party going
with his singing.'

I don't want to see Mum cry,
so I hug right back, even though
it's getting hard to hug her properly,
and then I go to my room.

I unfold the map of 'Leave Taking'.
It's getting a bit of farm dirt on it
and I like that. I have said goodbye
to almost every marked spot,
but there is one place left to go.
I roll up the map, tuck it into
my pocket and head around the back way
to go outside.

I just have time before some early neighbours
arrive to help out. I know there will be lots
of hugs and tears and cups of tea, coffee,
soft drinks, eating and storytelling.

Trigger has been dozing by his kennel and
he jumps up and follows me.

I wave to Dad putting some more stumps
onto the bonfire and keep walking
until I reach the oldest shed on the farm.
Pa called it the old black smithy shed.
Dad was going to knock it over with the
front-end loader, but I yelled and spluttered
and carried on, so he just shrugged his
shoulders and said, 'Alright son, maybe the O'Brien
family might restore it. Who knows?'

Pa said he could remember an old workman using
that shed when he was a boy.
'Always something breaking on a farm,
so it was handy to fix something yourself
or fashion a new part. Can't do that these days.'

This was one of Leah's favourite spots, even though
we had to make big stomping noises as we went
near it just in case
a snake or a rat was inside.
And we mainly went in winter. Such treasure,
Leah had said as we found old shrunken leather straps
from bridles and huge padded harnesses to put on the
Clydesdale horses that pulled the ploughs
before Great Grandpa had tractors.
Leah really liked the horseshoes
she found; some on nails on the wall,
others under layers of dirt on the earthen floor.

I know what I am looking for and I reach up
to take the smallest of all the horseshoes.
For a pony maybe or a magical tiny horse,
Leah had said. I will pack this with the gumnuts
and the map.

We'd made up games of cooking and feasts and wishing potions,
leaning over the bricked furnace, thinking
of the fierce heat and the sweat and the hammering.
Leah had gathered lots of horseshoe nails
in an old tin pot. But I leave those
for the next family.

Trigger is scratching in the corner.
'Come away,' I order. 'No time to chase anything now, we have to get back home. Tidy up.'

I go outside; already the sun is sinking.
Pa said he would wash down the yard for me tonight.

'Goodbye old black smithy shed,' I say.

Dad lights the bonfire.
It roars like a wild dragon.
People move back until the lick of flame
becomes less hungry.

Then the huge tree stumps
Dad has placed at the bottom,
with more at the top of the bonfire,
begin slow-burning.
I think of the box of Leah's drawings
and know that she'd like the ashes
left here.
The BBQ is already sizzling sausages,
hamburgers, chops.
Uncle Samuel is in charge.
He has a striped apron
on, a chef's hat and is waving
a huge pair of BBQ tongs.

He calls, 'Toby, has your mum got
any more onions?
Need more plates too.'
Then my friend Emmy comes over
and Jaxon joins her.
They follow me to the house.
In the kitchen they look at the little map
I placed on the noticeboard last night,
seeing that everyone in my family already knew
what I was doing.

'Places to say goodbye to,
this is my Leave Taking',
I've written in thick texta
and then drawn all the places
where I've camped so far.

Emmy smiles. 'Good idea Toby.'
Jaxon asks, 'What was it like camping
in each spot? Were you scared? I would be!'

And I smile for the first time tonight.
Somehow I don't care if my friends think
what I'm doing is weird,
not anymore.
But sometimes it's good to have friends agree.
'Only in the machinery shed,' I say,
then I tell them about the mice, the hessian bags
and lastly the snake.
'Yikes!' shouts Jaxon and he's jabbering on
about all the snake stories he knows
and I laugh.
Jaxon can be nearly as funny as Uncle Samuel.

I remember the errand I was running
for my uncle.
His wife, my Auntie Helen,
wipes her eyes as she hands me
a huge bowl of freshly chopped onions.
'Chopping onions always makes me cry,'
she says with a watery smile,

and Mum hugs her.
It's good Mum has some friends
with her too.

I show Emmy where the plates are
and we race back out to the BBQ.
We line up like everyone else
for salad, bread, meat.
Then our friends show what they've been cooking
all afternoon.
The slices, cakes, pavs and cheesecakes.

'Wow!' Jaxon lines up for seconds and thirds.
Then Mum brings out lemon meringue pie.
'Leah's favourite,' is all she says.

Soon we are all full.
Trigger is having a ball,
jumping for meat scraps,
wagging his tail so hard that it scrapes

the dirt and pushes puffs of dust into the night air.
Uncle Samuel is trying to get Trigger
to roll over before he gives him a scrap of meat.

But the cats hide; they don't like strangers.

Jaxon's dad
cleans up the BBQ,
and Uncle Samuel sits and begins to tune his guitar.

Soon he's singing and we're joining in.
An owl flies from the old sugar gums.
And the bonfire hisses
and smoke curls up as high
as the night stars. It's like tinsel tonight,
and away towards the south there is a small
seam of light from the nearest town.

We are leaving.

Goodbye cowshed, machinery shed,
hayshed, chook pen, old red truck,
Memorial Hill, old black smithy shed,
blue wrens, magpies.
Goodbye sugar gums, White Tail, Streak,
kingfishers, dam, old pig sties, dairy cows,
tree house, galahs, old mother cat,
deep well, fruit trees …
I run out of special things to farewell.

Emmy and Jaxon curl up on the cushions and rugs
Mum has placed away from the fire
and Shelley creeps softly to Emmy.
I lie down near Trigger and close my eyes.
Uncle Samuel has stopped playing and singing.
Jaxon's dad is talking to Dad,
putting a hand on his shoulder
and Mum is surrounded by neighbours
talking softly. I hear Leah's name,
my name, but I am drifting.

Pa puts a rug around me and later
I hear cars starting up, someone shovelling all
the stray bits of wood and ash back into
the still-burning bonfire.
I hear Auntie Helen say, 'I'll help wash those dishes.'
Dad lifts me and carries me
to my bed. I feel his kiss on my forehead,
and then I am asleep.

Next morning, Uncle Samuel is cooking bacon
and eggs. He and Auntie Helen are
helping with the shift today, organising the boxes
already stacked for when the removal van comes to
the house,
and the semitrailer
for the beef cattle,
and a truck for the tractors we are taking.

'Great evening Toby!' grins Uncle Samuel.
'Hey, love the map you made. I was reading it
while you were still snoozing. Can't say
I remember half those places on the farm,
but then I was never a farmer like your dad.
Leah would have loved your map.'
'Yes, she would Toby,' smiles Mum warmly.
I haven't seen Mum smile like that for a long time.
'The map was a great idea.
I've been too caught up with grief for Leah
to help you through this.'
Mum comes to give me
my good morning hug.
'But Dad and I can't stay here any longer.
We need a fresh start,
need to make new memories.'

Dad walks in then, still in his work clothes
and smelling like the cowshed. But comes straight
over and hugs me.

And there we are with bacon sizzling, the smell
of cow manure on Dad's clothes,
Auntie Helen smiling at us
and Uncle Samuel yelling out,
'Hold it. This will make a great photo.'
And he snaps us just like that
in the middle of our last morning here
on Deep Well Farm. Trigger comes
charging in; he senses something.
And Pa walks in. He smells like
smoke from the bonfire. 'Just dampening
down the coals – lots of rubbish still burning.
It was the biggest bonfire I've seen.'
And I know I need to record that on my map.
I take it down from the wall and write,
then I place it in my backpack.
'Can't forget it,' I say.

'Well, that was the last milking.
The O'Briens will take over for tonight's milking.'

And I know it has been just as hard for Dad
to decide to shift.
Mum hugs me tighter and
I feel the large swell of the new baby
growing in her tummy.

'Toby, after we go to our new farm,
in a few weeks' time you will have a brother.
We haven't had much time to talk about
the coming baby,
but I thought you could help me choose some
drawings
of Leah's to make a mural for his room.
What do you think?'

I don't know whether to pull away
or hug more.
Instead, I take a deep breath
and say, 'Leah would have liked that.'
And suddenly I realise that I would like that too.

Then Uncle Samuel starts singing,
Trigger barks,
the kettle whistles furiously
and Pa says, 'I can hear the first truck coming off
the highway. Better get some breakfast down.'

And we all sit and Auntie Helen is talking about
making a patchwork quilt for the baby,
and Pa leans across to me
and says, 'We won't be leaving Leah behind,
she will be coming with us,' and he gently punches
his chest, right where his heart is beating.

'Here's something for you,' says Uncle Samuel
as he ruffles my hair, just like my dad does.
'Your mum told me about your
Leave Taking map on the phone the other day,
so I thought you might like to write in this
and call it "Making a New Beginning". Well, just a
suggestion.'

And he chuckles as I pull the wrapping paper away
from a thick notebook.

As I eat my toast I open up the book
and write:

'Our goodbyes are nearly done.
But we'll never leave Leah.
She will always be with us.'

I take out my texta and add a thick smiling mouth.
Leah would have liked that.

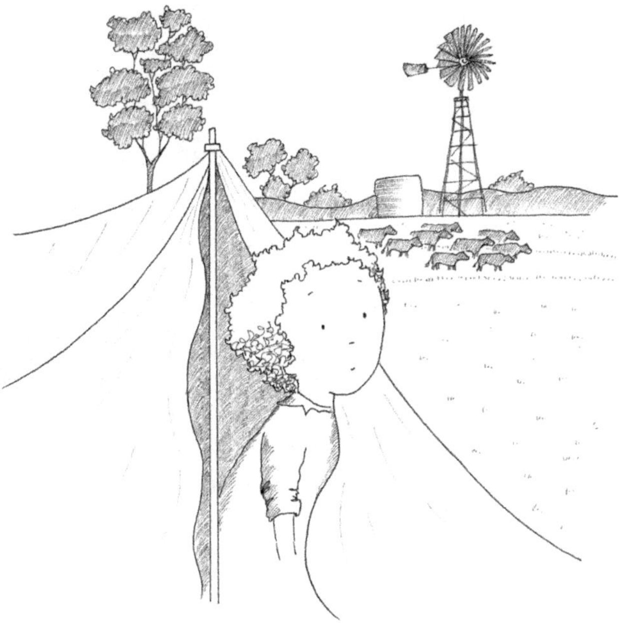

Acknowledgements

Of course a family, my family, is the inspiration for many of my stories. This particular book mirrors, to some extent, the leave taking of our own farm life, and my adjusting to living with a cancer diagnosis. I experienced a deep satisfaction in melding the two together in a story for anyone needing to come to terms with a farewell of their own. But inspiration is only the initial part of the writing and I have some very important people to thank for their support and encouragement throughout the book's growth.

To my wonderful editors at UQP who loved this story enough to guide, suggest and inspire me again to flesh out Toby's story even more. Thanks Kristina Schulz and Vanessa Pellatt.

To Peter Carnavas who has brought Toby and Trigger to immediate visual life, thank you.

To my agent Jane Novak for her encouraging support and belief in my writing.

To a residency in Brisbane in 2016 through the May Gibbs Children's Literature Trust Fellowship for allowing the words and tears to grow into a manuscript. Special thanks to Judy Russell.

To my husband Kelvin, to my big supportive family, to the little dog who lies at my feet, to Katrina Nannestad and my writing friends – thank you.

Hard journeys often come to an end at a startling new destination.

Leave Taking is such a destination.

Lorraine Marwood was born and raised in rural Victoria and lived with her husband and their six children on a dairy farm. She has twelve grandchildren and loves to craft, sew, garden, walk her dog Monti and bake for family gatherings. She has been a headmistress of a rural school and has studied literacy. Early in her writing journey, she wrote poetry for literary magazines in Australia and overseas. Lorraine has published several children's novels and collections of poetry and won the inaugural Prime Minister's Literary Award for children's fiction in 2010 for her novel *Star Jumps*. She has enjoyed three fellowships with the May Gibbs Children's Literature Trust.

Leave Taking was the joint winner of the 2019 NSW Premier's Literary Awards, Patricia Wrightson Prize for Children's Literature and was shortlisted for the 2019 CBCA Book of the Year, Younger Readers.

www.lorrainemarwood.com

Tree house
Machinery shed
Old black smithy shed
Bonfire
Old red truck
Hayshed
Old pig sties